ENEMY

BY

SAMUEL OYENIYI

DEDICATION

Enemy is dedicated to God and everyone who made this work a success in their diverse ways.

It is also dedicated to anyone and everyone who is trying to crack or has cracked the code to emotional intelligence as a broad topic.

TABLE OF CONTENTS

ACKNOWLEDGEMENT

I acknowledge God, my family, the team at Heritage Radio, Heritage Polytechnic, Eket, AKS, Nigeria and the team at Author's Arsenal who collectively made this work a reality.

Thank you!

PREFACE

Enemy is a story that revolves around the flaws and fragile ties in family, friendship, and society at large, as well as the various ways we can confront and manage them. At its heart is the Thompson family, who live in one of the most popular estates in town.

Janet, the main character, and her best friend, Bella, stand out as the most successful working-class women in their respective families. But after attending a company anniversary, events take a turn that will test loyalty, love, and the meaning of trust.

CHAPTER ONE – THE THOMPSONS

The slam of the front door echoed through the Thompson home. Michael barged in, flinging his bag to the floor. His frustration was almost tangible.

"I just hate this country," he muttered bitterly. "It's so bad and poor."

From across the room, Godwin burst into laughter, his voice filling the parlour.

Michael narrowed his eyes. "And what's funny? Because I said it's bad and poor?"

"Your tone," Godwin chuckled. "The way you stormed in... everything about you this whole week. Get yourself together, please."

Michael's scowl deepened. "Sometimes I regret having you as a brother."

"Don't be angry, I was joking," Godwin replied quickly.

On the long sofa, Janet had been quietly watching the exchange. Unable to hold it in any longer, she laughed softly. "Men will always be men," she sighed.

Michael turned to her sharply. "And what does that mean?"

"That men will always be men," she repeated with a mischievous glint.

He shook his head. "I thought you wanted to say something meaningful."

"Don't mind her," Godwin added. "She's always saying nonsense."

"I was just—" Janet began.

"Just what?" Godwin snapped.

"She doesn't have anything to say," Michael cut in. "Don't bother."

Janet raised her hands lightly. "We're not fighting, anyway."

Michael sighed, picked up his bag, and muttered, "I'll see you guys later."

CHAPTER TWO –
A CALL TO BELLA

Friday mornings usually buzzed with life, but today the roads looked unusually quiet. Janet frowned as she stared out the window. "Strange," she murmured. "I hope nothing is happening today. I didn't hear of anything."

Shaking off the thought, she picked up her phone and dialed her best friend.

"Hi, Bella," she said warmly.

Bella's laughter rang through the line. "Hello. Today looks somehow oo."

"How does it look somehow?" Janet asked, curious.

"Because this is the first time you're calling me so early—on a Friday, for that matter!"

"Ah ah, so I can't call my best friend again?" Janet teased.

"Of course you can. I'm just surprised."

"Well, I wanted to invite you to a party."

"A party? What party?"

"It's actually an anniversary—my company's anniversary."

Bella gasped in delight. "Wow! I'd really love to be there."

Janet raised a brow. "You would love to? What do you mean—you're not coming?"

"I am!" Bella assured her quickly. "I just meant I want to be there, you know... meet new people and all. I'll surely come."

"Thanks so much. I really appreciate it."

"You're welcome. What are best friends for?" Bella laughed.

The two women chuckled together before Janet reminded her, "It starts at 4 p.m."

"No problem, I'll be there," Bella promised.

CHAPTER THREE – THE ANNIVERSARY

By mid-afternoon, Bella was already waiting outside Janet's home, leaning casually on her car door while swinging her keys.

Janet hurried out, slightly flustered. "I'm so sorry, but you didn't call."

"There's no problem," Bella smiled. "Shall we?"

Together, they drove to Octagon Company Ltd. The building stood proudly, its decorations glowing under the soft evening sun. From the exterior to the interior, the event planner's brilliance was evident.

Inside, Bella paused, her eyes widening. "I'm shocked," she whispered. "The last time I came, most structures weren't completed. I'm just happy for you, that's all."

Janet's face lit up. "I had to put in more effort. We even had staff before the completion."

"That's impressive," Bella nodded.

The main hall was massive—thirty thousand seats filled with guests moving about. Yellow and blue lined the walls, with paintings in strategic corners whispering their own silent messages.

Bella exhaled in admiration. "Janet, your company is massive and beautifully decorated. Not everyone who owns a company manages it this well."

Janet chuckled. "Is it not meant to be decorated?"

"Don't get me wrong," Bella continued passionately. "It's frustrating seeing others celebrate two or three years with nothing to show. Meanwhile, look at yours—ten years strong."

Janet laughed again. "Calm down, abeg."

"Don't even tell me that," Bella said firmly. "You won't understand."

"I do," Janet said gently.

"Hadiza Bella Enterprise," Bella muttered. "The name is fine, but not as fine as its reality."

Janet chuckled. "It even has your name attached to it."

Bella rolled her eyes. "Don't go there."

"Okay, I'm sorry."

CHAPTER FOUR – VICTOR ROWLAND

As they spoke, Bella's gaze drifted toward a man seated at the bar. Their eyes locked for a moment before she quickly looked away, her unease not escaping Janet's notice.

"Is there a problem, Bella?"

"No, not really," Bella stammered.

Janet frowned. "You look worried. Are you sure you're okay?"

"I'm fine," Bella insisted.

Moments later, the man approached, hand in pocket, steps deliberate.

"I hope I'm not interrupting," he said politely.

"No, you're not," Janet replied. "Is there any problem?"

"Not at all. My name is Victor Rowland. May I know you?"

"Janet Thompson," she said, shaking his hand.

"And you are?" he asked, turning to Bella.

"Bella. Just call me Bella," she replied nervously.

"She doesn't like giving her full name," Janet teased.

"Of course I know," Rowland said, eyes glinting.

Janet's brows furrowed. "Wait... you know each other?"

"Not exactly," Rowland replied. "We've just met on different occasions."

"That's nice," Janet smiled.

"Would you mind if we had a drink?" he asked.

"All of us?" Bella asked quickly.

"Sure," Rowland said.

The trio made their way to the bar.

CHAPTER FIVE – SECRETS

After ordering Chapman for them all, Rowland leaned in. "What I have to say concerns someone very close to you, Janet."

Her heart skipped. "Hope there's no problem."

"There is," he said gravely. "Something that could cost you your company."

Janet froze. "What? How? What are you talking about?"

His gaze flickered toward Bella. "Your friend. Leaving office keys in the hands of someone close to her is very dangerous."

Janet's chest tightened. "I've suspected her since I invited her for this ceremony. But... she's my best friend."

Rowland's voice was firm. "Best friend indeed. Protect your company. Your documents are not safe."

Janet's eyes darted with doubt. "Why should I trust you? We've only just met."

"You don't have to," Rowland said coldly. "Suit yourself. But I'm available if you need me."

He walked away, leaving Janet trembling.

Moments later, she rushed into her office. The sound of hurried footsteps reached Bella, who scrambled to shove documents into an envelope. But they slipped from her hands and scattered across the floor—just as Janet opened the door.

Janet's scream pierced the room. "Oh my God! Bella!"

She dropped to the ground, staring in disbelief as the papers lay exposed in Bella's trembling hands.

From the corner, Rowland's voice cut like a knife: "Best friend indeed."

He raised his phone, snapping a picture of the scene.